TIMELESS TALES

Myths

Retold by TANA REIFF

Illustrated by SHERRY KRUGGEL

SIGNAL HILL™

PUBLICATIONS

ATTENTION READERS: We would like to hear what you think about our books. Please send your comments or suggestions to:

Signal Hill Publications
P.O. Box 131
Syracuse, NY 13210-0131

• • •

SIGNAL HILL™

PUBLICATIONS

ISBN 0-88336-272-4

© 1991 Signal Hill Publications
A publishing imprint of Laubach Literacy International
Box 131, Syracuse, New York 13210-0131

Printed in the United States of America

Project editor: Elizabeth Costello
Manuscript editor: Mark Legler
Designer: Patricia Rapple
Illustrator: Sherry Kruggel
Cover design: The WD Burdick Company
Sponsoring editor: Marianne Ralbovsky

10 9 8 7 6 5 4

Signal Hill is a not-for-profit publisher. The proceeds from the sale of this book support the national and international programs of Laubach Literacy International.

Contents

Introduction

In the early days of every land, people told stories to help them understand their world. Sometimes all those stories put together became the people's religion.

So it was with the people of early Greece. These people told many wonderful stories to explain how the world came about and how things worked. These stories were called *myths*.

Myths were all about two main groups: *gods* and *mortals*. The gods and goddesses looked like people but had magic powers and never died. They lived on a mountain in the heavens called Olympus (oh-LIM-pus). Their leader was named Zeus (ZOOSE). The gods and goddesses often played tricks on the mortals, or common men and women. So the mortals lived in fear of the gods and did their best not to anger them. Some mortals did very amazing things and were called *heroes*.

Are the myths true? Many of the stories are based on real events. Many others are not. Some are partly real and partly not real. Perhaps they don't really explain how the world came about and how things work. But almost all the myths teach us something about human nature.

Pandora's Box

At one time, there were men on earth but no women. Zeus asked for the gods' help in making the first woman. The son of Zeus took some clay and gave the woman a shape. The Four Winds blew life into her. Aphrodite (AFF-row-DIE-tee), the goddess of love and beauty, gave the woman soft skin and a pretty smell and filled her with love. Athena (uh-THEEN-uh), the goddess of wisdom, gave the woman a strong mind. Hera (HAIR-uh), the queen of the gods, made her curious. The woman would always want to know about things.

The first woman had everything. The gods named her Pandora (pan-DOOR-uh). This means "the gift of all." Then they gave her to a mortal named Epimetheus (EPP-uh-MEE-thee-us), to be his wife. Along with Pandora came a box. It was a gift to her new husband from the gods. They did not tell Pandora what was inside.

Epimetheus and Pandora fell very much in love. "Why should I be so lucky?" Epimetheus wondered. "Why should the gods give me such a perfect woman?"

"Please don't ask such questions," said Pandora. "Just open the box. I want to see my gift to you."

"No," said Epimetheus. "I don't trust the gods. We must never open the box. It may be a trick."

So the box stayed closed.

But Pandora grew more and more curious as to what was inside it. One day Epimetheus was away. "I must see what is in the box," Pandora said to herself. "I will only look inside. I will not touch a thing."

She slowly lifted the lid of the box. Out flew all sorts of ugly monsters. Sickness, Sadness, and Hate flew out of the box and into the world. Pandora banged down the lid as fast as she could. But all the bad things were already loose. Now the world would just have to live with them.

When Epimetheus got home, Pandora told
him what she had done. He was very sad to
hear the news. He went over to the box.
"Listen!" he said. "I hear a noise. Something
else is still in there. Go ahead and lift the lid
again. Surely, nothing could be worse than
what already flew out."

Pandora lifted the lid. There, at the bottom, was Hope. It, too, flew out of the box and into the world.

This was just what the world needed. The people would have many bad things to deal with. But now, no matter what happened, there would always be Hope.

Midas and the Golden Touch

 Midas (MY-dus) was a greedy man who happened to be a king. He ruled over the Land of the Roses. It was called that because so many roses grew there.

One day, King Midas found a man under a rose bush. "Where did you come from?" Midas asked the man.

"I was at a party with Bacchus (BAHK-us), the god of wine," answered the man. "I must be lost."

King Midas led the man inside. He took care of him for 10 days. Then he sent him back to Bacchus.

The wine god was always happy to get people back. "Thank you!" he told Midas. "For your trouble, you may make a wish. Wish for anything you want!"

"I want everything I touch to turn to gold," King Midas said.

"It shall be done!" said Bacchus.

King Midas couldn't believe his good luck. How wonderful! All he had to do was touch something and it would turn to gold! Midas looked forward to becoming very rich.

He sat down to eat his dinner. He picked up his fork. As soon as his fingers touched it, it turned to gold. "Who needs silver forks when I can have gold?" Midas laughed.

Then he picked up a piece of bread. It, too, turned to gold. Midas started to put the bread in his mouth. But it was gold. He couldn't eat gold!

He picked up his glass to take a drink. The glass turned to gold. And as soon as the water touched his mouth, it also turned to gold.

"Daughter! Daughter!" he called to his dear child. "Help me! Everything I touch turns to gold!"

He reached out to the young girl. Sure enough, she turned to gold. She froze in place. She couldn't move. It was as if she were dead.

"Oh, dear!" cried Midas. "Now I've really done it." He looked up to the sky. "Please, oh please, Bacchus! Take my wish away! I am hungry and thirsty! I have lost my daughter! I don't want everything to turn to gold!"

Bacchus heard Midas crying. "Go down to the river," said Bacchus. "Wash yourself in the clear water. Your wish will wash away. Then pour the water of the river on your daughter. You will have her back."

Midas did as Bacchus told him. When he touched the grass by the river, it did not turn to gold. It stayed as green as grass should be. The terrible wish was gone! But for years after, people found gold along the river where Midas had washed.

Narcissus and Echo

Echo (ECK-oh) was a young woman who talked all the time. Zeus's wife, Hera, couldn't stand to hear Echo talking so much. So she put a spell on her. "You will never be able to speak first," Hera told Echo. "You will only be able to repeat what is said to you."

This was very hard on a person who loved to talk. Echo would open her mouth, but nothing would come out. However, when someone else finished speaking, she would repeat what was said.

Now, all the young women were in love
with a young man named Narcissus (nar-
SIS-iss). To be sure, he had a beautiful face.
However, Narcissus had a cold heart. The
women all ran after him, but he never even
looked at them. He just ran away.

Echo, too, fell in love with Narcissus. With
Hera's spell on her, she could not speak
first. One day she followed him through the
woods. Narcissus heard her behind him. He
turned around. He saw no one. "Is someone
here?" he called.

"Here," answered Echo, who could only
repeat what he said.

"What do you want if I find you?" asked
Narcissus.

"You," answered Echo.

"I will die before I love you," warned Narcissus.

"I love you," answered Echo.

This went on and on until Narcissus had had enough. He went along his way and left Echo behind.

Echo felt very sad. Like all the other women, she could not catch Narcissus. She went off to a cave and melted away. Only her voice was left. You can still hear her if you call.

The gods on Mount Olympus saw what had happened. They decided it was time for Narcissus to learn a lesson about love. He would find out how it felt to love someone without return.

Here is how it happened. Narcissus bent down to take a drink of water from a pond. As good-looking as he was, this was the first time he had ever seen himself. "Look at that beautiful face!" he cried to the face in the pond. His cold heart melted. He tried to touch the face in the water. But when he did, the water moved and the face went away.

Time and time again, Narcissus tried to get close to the face in the water. Time and time again, it went away without a word.

"Now I know how the young women feel when I run away from them," said Narcissus.

He was so sad. He never left that spot by the pond. Narcissus was in love. He began to waste away. As he was dying, he called out "Good-bye" to the face in the water. "Good-bye," came the sound of Echo from the cave.

The next spring, there was nothing left of Narcissus. But on the spot where he had sat grew a new, white flower. These flowers still grow today. They are named after Narcissus.

Flying
to the
Sun

Daedalus (DED-uh-luss) was a bright man. He was full of ideas on how to build and make new things. His king asked him to build a life-sized maze. The king put people inside the maze, hoping they would never find their way out.

But some people did find their way out of the maze. The king believed that Daedalus had told them how. So he put Daedalus and his son Icarus (ICK-uh-russ) into the maze to see if they could find their way out.

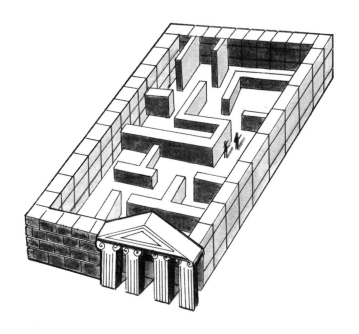

The father and son walked and walked
in the maze. Before long they hit a dead
end. They tried again, and again they hit
a dead end.

"Are we stuck in here for the rest of our
lives?" cried Icarus.

Daedalus raised his eyes to the blue sky
above. "I am thinking of a way to escape," he
said. "We might be stopped by land or water.
But the air and the sky are free. The only way
out of here is up. Son, we must fly out!"

"But we are not birds," said Icarus. "How
can we fly?"

Daedalus worked out a plan. Each day, they caught a bird. They took two feathers from each bird. That way, the bird could still fly. Day by day, the pile of feathers grew.

Together the father and son used the feathers to make wings. They got some wax from the bees that made their home in the maze. They stuck the wings together with the wax. Soon, they tried out their new wings.

"This is great!" called the boy as he flew low to the ground. "We are like the birds!"

"Be careful!" called back Daedalus to his son. "We can't fly too close to the sun. The heat from the sun will melt the wax, and our wings will fall apart."

But, like many young people, Icarus did not listen to his father. Each day, he flew a little higher. The wings stayed in place. "See, Father!" laughed Icarus. "I am flying close to the sun, and everything is fine!"

At last, the day came to fly out of the maze and away to a safe place.

"I warn you!" said Daedalus as they rose toward the sky. "Do not fly so close to the sun!"

But Icarus only flew closer than ever to the sun and its heat. As he did, the wax began to melt. One by one, the feathers fell off. Before long, his wings fell apart. Icarus fell down, down, down. Daedalus could not help his son. Icarus dropped into the sea. The water covered him, and he was gone.

Daedalus flew on. He made it to a safe land where he lived for many years. But he was sad for the rest of his days.

The Trojan War:
The Fairest of All

 Early Greece is probably most famous for a long and bloody war. The war took place between Greece and the city of Troy. It was called the Trojan War. Here is how it began.

Up on Mount Olympus, the gods and goddesses were having a party. A rather mean goddess named Eris (EAR-iss) was not asked to the party. This made her very angry. So Eris waited outside the party with a golden apple in her hand. On it she wrote, "For the fairest." She threw the apple into the middle of the party.

Each goddess believed she was the fairest. All of them wanted the apple. The gods at the party decided that one of three goddesses must be the fairest. These were Hera, Athena, and Aphrodite. Hera was queen of the gods and the wife of Zeus. Athena was the goddess of wisdom and the daughter of Zeus. Aphrodite was the goddess of love and beauty.

"You pick among us," the three goddesses begged Zeus. "Who is the fairest of us all?"

"You are all beautiful," said Zeus. "I will not choose. There is a fine young man named Paris. He is the son of King Priam (PRY-um) of Troy. I shall send the three of you to him. He will decide who should get the golden apple."

Paris was off in the hills keeping his father's sheep. The king had sent him there because the gods had told him that Troy would be destroyed because of Paris. The king felt it was best to send his son away.

What a surprise for Paris when three goddesses appeared before him! They did not ask him who was the fairest. Rather, each goddess told him what she would give him if he picked her.

"I will give you all of Europe and Asia," promised Hera, the queen of the gods.

"I will give you the mind to win a war someday!" promised Athena, the goddess of wisdom.

"I will give you the fairest woman in the world!" promised Aphrodite, the goddess of love.

Paris did not want power or wisdom.
He wanted love. He gave the golden apple
to Aphrodite.

"The fairest woman is Helen," she said.
"She is married to Menelaus (MEN-uh-LAY-us),
the king of the Greek city of Sparta."

Paris headed for Sparta. He did not know
then about a promise made among the men
of Greece.

The promise came about when Helen's
father was trying to choose her husband. She
was so beautiful that her father was afraid.
If he chose one man, the others would be
angry. They might go to war against the one
he chose.

So all the men made a promise. All of them would help Helen's husband if anyone tried to steal her away. Helen married Menelaus. The other men kept their promise. They would help him if he needed it.

When Paris got to Sparta, he went to visit Helen and Menelaus. They brought him into their home and were very nice to him. Then Menelaus had to go away. While he was gone, Paris and Helen fell in love and ran away together.

When Menelaus returned, his beautiful wife was gone. He called upon the men of Greece to help him get her back. They all set off for Troy to find Paris and bring Helen home. Paris had no idea what his city would have to face. His love for Helen would start a war.

The Trojan War:
Achilles' Heel

The war between Troy and Greece began. There were battles on land and sea. Both sides fought so hard that the war went on for 10 years. Yet in all this time, the Greeks could not get into the city of Troy. A high wall ran all around the city, and the Greeks could not get by it.

The great hero of the Greek army was Achilles (uh-KILL-eez). He was strong and brave, and everyone knew it. He had won many battles for the Greeks.

As strong as he was, however, Achilles had a weak spot. When he was a baby, his mother dipped him into a magic river. The water from this river would keep Achilles safe from all harm. However, when his mother dipped him, she held him by the place just above his right heel. The magic water did not touch that spot. Achilles' heel was the one place he could be hurt.

At Troy, Achilles had fought one-on-one
against Hector, the son of King Priam of Troy
and the brother of Paris. But these fights
were always outside the wall. Even Achilles
could not get past.

One last battle took place between Achilles and Hector. It was a sword fight. Achilles knocked Hector's sword out of his hands. Then he chased Hector all around the city wall. At last, he caught Hector and killed him. Then Achilles tied Hector's body behind his chariot. He ordered his horses to run. They dragged Hector's body behind the chariot in the dirt and dust.

King Priam was very sad to hear of Hector's death. He begged for the return of his son's body. What harm could there be in doing that? Achilles said to himself. So he brought Hector's body to the city gate of Troy. He did not know that Paris was waiting for him at the gate.

Achilles lifted Hector's body from the chariot. Just then, Paris shot an arrow at Achilles. The arrow hit Achilles in his right heel. This, of course, was his weak spot. The arrow killed him right away.

The Trojan War:
The Wooden Horse

 After Achilles died, another great hero rose up in the Greek army. His name was Odysseus (oh-DISS-e-us). He was king of Ithaca, but he fought like everyone else.

"There is only one way we can win over the Trojans," said Odysseus. "We must get past the gate and into the city."

"But how?" the other men wondered. "We can't get in the gate. And we can't break down the wall."

Odysseus asked Athena, the goddess of wisdom, what they should do.

Athena told him a poem:

> *Could is should,*
>
> *Should is would,*
>
> *Would is wood, of course.*
>
> *What began with an apple*
>
> *Must end with a horse.*

What could this mean? Odysseus wondered.
He knew about the golden apple that had
started the Trojan War. But what was this
about a horse? Then it came to him. He must
build a wooden horse!

Odysseus worked out a plan. He and his
men built a huge wooden horse. It was so big
that 20 men could fit inside it. There was a
trap door in the belly of the horse. There
were wheels under its feet.

The next morning, the Trojans looked over their wall. There were no Greeks in sight. Where could they be? The Trojans believed the war must be over. They believed the Greeks had given up and gone home.

Then the Trojans saw the wooden horse outside the gate. They believed the Greeks were leaving them a gift of peace.

"Beware of Greeks bearing gifts," King Priam's helper said. "They could be playing a trick."

But King Priam opened the gate. A group of men rolled the horse into the city. There it sat as the Trojans went to sleep. They slept well, believing they had won the war and peace had come at last.

But in the middle of the night, the trap door in the horse opened. Out came the 20 Greeks. Among them were Odysseus and Menelaus. They all ran toward the city gate and opened it wide.

The rest of the Greek army had not really gone home. They had sailed in their boats, just out of sight of Troy.

During the night they sailed back and waited on land. When the gate opened, the army rushed into Troy.

The Trojans did not have a chance. The Greeks killed everyone in sight. Then they set the city on fire. Soon, there was nothing left of Troy.

Some say Paris was killed in this last battle of the war. Others say he got away and lived out the rest of his days with another name in another land.

Aphrodite, the goddess of love and beauty, came to Troy. She had helped start the war. Now she helped Menelaus get his wife, Helen, out of Troy. The two of them went back to Sparta. For the rest of their days, they lived a happy life as king and queen.

After 10 years, the Trojan War was over. Odysseus and the rest of the Greek army began their long trip home.

Oedipus and the Riddle of the Sphinx

Oedipus (ED-uh-pus) was born to Queen Jocasta (jo-CAST-uh) and King Laius (LAY-us) in the city of Thebes (THEEBZ). When Oedipus was born, the gods told Laius he would be killed by his own son. The son would then marry his own mother. Laius felt he had to get rid of the boy. So he sent the baby Oedipus up to a mountain. There he was left to die.

But Oedipus did not die. He grew to be a man. He lived his life alone and sad.

One day he heard about something called the Sphinx (SFINKS). This was a monster with the head of a woman, the body of a lion, and wings like a bird. Near Thebes, the Sphinx lay in wait for people to walk by. Then she would ask them a riddle. If they could not answer the riddle, she would eat them. No one got past because no one could give the right answer.

Oedipus decided to try the riddle of the Sphinx. On his way, he came across a band of four men. One of them hit Oedipus with a stick. To save himself, Oedipus killed three of the four men. Then he went on toward the Sphinx.

At last he reached the monster. "Here is the riddle," the Sphinx said. "What goes on four legs in the morning, two at noon, and three at night?"

"That's easy," answered Oedipus. "The answer is man. As a child he crawls on hands and knees. When he grows up, he walks on two legs. And when he is old he walks with a cane."

This answer was right. The Sphinx let Oedipus pass. After that, the Sphinx ate no more people. The people of Thebes were saved.

When Oedipus got to Thebes, King Laius had just died. The people made Oedipus the king, and he married Queen Jocasta.

Years later, Thebes had more trouble. There was not enough food and not enough clean water. Many people got sick. Many of them died.

The people asked the gods for help. "You must find the person who killed King Laius," they were told. "When that person is out of Thebes, all will be well again."

As king, Oedipus wanted the killer to be found. So he asked the wisest man in Thebes to help him find that person. "That person is you," the old man said.

"That is a crazy idea!" said Queen Jocasta. "Laius was killed by a robber. It happened at the place where three roads come together."

"When did this happen?" asked Oedipus.

"Not long before you came to Thebes," said Queen Jocasta. "Laius was with three other men. All but one of them were killed. The one who got away came back to tell the story."

"The place where three roads come together?" cried Oedipus. "That is where I was hit with a stick. That is where I killed three of four men."

Then they put it all together. What the gods had said when Oedipus was born had come true! Oedipus had killed his father and married his own mother. He did not mean to do either. But that is what happened.

Oedipus stepped down as King of Thebes. Queen Jocasta's brother took over the throne and the country.

And so Oedipus had not only answered the riddle of the Sphinx. He had found the answer to the puzzle of his whole life.